JELLYBEANS

Declan—
Be the best Jellybean
you can be! ☺
Kiersten Hall

written by kiersten hall
illustrated by shaina ryther
designed by chelsea farr

www.khallbooks.com

Library of Congress Cataloging-in-Publication Data
Hall, Kiersten L., author.
Ryther, Shaina M., illustrator.
Farr, Chelsea M., designer.
JELLYBEANS / Kiersten L. Hall. - First edition.
Summary: Illustrations accompanied by a poem about jellybeans
who celebrate their unique qualities together and teach children about kindness and inclusivity.
ISBN 978-1-7337717-2-6 (paperback) - ISBN 978-1-7337717-3-3 (hardcover)
[1. Fiction. 2. Children's fiction. 3. Stories in rhyme. 4.Poetry for children.]
Library of Congress Control Number: 2019904023

Printed and bound in the United States of America
First printing June 2019

People are like jellybeans, wouldn't you agree?

So many different kinds!
Let us look and see.

Cinnamon is sassy

2

and
Chocolate
Pudding
is lumpy.

French
Vanilla
is
artistic,

4

while
Sour Cherry
is grumpy!

5

Tutti Frutti
is
fun
and
groovy,

6

Grapefruit is refreshing and tart!

7

Toasty Marshmallow is light-hearted and mellow,

Mango Chili is a wanderer **at heart.**

Tangerine,
Orange,
Lemon,
Lime...

10

All kissed by the sun
and having a great time.

11

**Coconut is flaky
and a little outer-spacey,**

Kiwi
is
hip
and
cool.

Pomegranate is curious and mysterious,

and
Pineapple
plays
the
fool.

Licorice is dapper,

Cantaloupe
is
wise.

17

Watermelon is earthy,

18

Pear

is full of surprise!

Raspberry, Cherry,
Blackberry, Blue...

Mango, Cranberry, and Plum for you!

21

Buttery
Popcorn
is comforting,

22

Bubblegum is snappy and loud!

23

While **Banana** plays to a crowd.

25

Red Apple,
Green Apple...
Different, but the same.

STARRING

CARAMEL POPCORN AND COTTON CANDY

"IT'S ALL IN THE NAME!"

27

Have a look around. No need to be shy.

Who are you and who am I?

Are you

snappy

and

loud

or

mysterious

and

cool?

All of us are different.
Our personalities vary.

So do our
shapes, sizes,
and colors.

Just look at these
singing berries!

33

Orange and blue,
pink and green...

There are more colors than you've ever seen!

Large and oblong,
or tiny and small...

We're in this together, one and all.

Much like a dish of jellybeans, each of us brings a different flavor.

These
differences
of ours are
something
we should
savor.

Be
kind
to
everyone.

Don't be a bully.

Instead, be a **friend**.

Accept others fully.

Delight in being **smooth**, groovy, or **dapper**.

Celebrate everyone else, too!

42

Whether you're spacey, shy, or feeling blue,

it's alright to just be you.

Our differences make us special -
all of us, near and far.

44

Be your own jellybean.
Be proud of who you are!

45

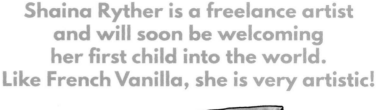
Shaina Ryther is a freelance artist
and will soon be welcoming
her first child into the world.
Like French Vanilla, she is very artistic!

Kiersten Hall is an
independent author
and mother of four.
She is also fun and groovy,
like Tutti Frutti.

Chelsea Farr
is a graphic artist
and proud dog mom.
She couldn't decide on a jellybean,
but seems partial to berry flavors.

CPSIA information can be obtained at www.ICGtesting.com
Printed in the USA
BVIW121717260919
559527BV00006B/9